# The Journey of an Eagle

A triumph story and compilation of poetry describing the victory over molestation, battery, physical and emotional abuse

WRITTEN BY
## KAREN MARIE BERARD MIÑO

PROISLE PUBLISHING

© COPYRIGHT 2024 BY KAREN MARIE BERARD MIÑO

ISBN: 978-1-963735-97-0

All rights reserved. No part of this book may be reproduced or transmitted in any form or by any means, electronic or mechanical, including photocopying, recording, or by any information storage and retrieval system, without permission in writing from the copyright owner.

The views expressed in this work are solely those of the author and do not necessarily reflect the views of the publisher, and the publisher disclaims any responsibility for them.

**To order additional copies of this book, contact:**

Proisle Publishing Services LLC
39-67 58th Street, 1st floor
Woodside, NY 11377, USA
Phone: (+1 646-480-0129)
info@proislepublishing.com

# Table of Content

| | |
|---|---:|
| **THE JOURNEY OF AN EAGLE** | 1 |
| **THE KITE AND THE HOLDER OF THE KITE THAT WE ARE**<br>January 12, 1998 | 2 |
| **UNSAFE TOUCH TO HEALING TOUCH** | 4 |
| **JIMMY**<br>December 6, 1990 | 8 |
| **RUNNING AWAY**<br>September 25, 1990 | 9 |
| **MOTHER HELP ME**<br>September 25, 1990 | 10 |
| **A CHILD'S EYES**<br>December 23, 1988 | 11 |
| **PROGRESSION**<br>December 26, 1988 | 12 |
| **LIGHT OVERCOMES DARKNESS**<br>July 14, 1999 | 13 |
| **OLD HABITS ARE HARD TO BREAK**<br>December 28, 1988 | 15 |
| **VESSELS OF THE LORD**<br>DECEMBER 29, 1998 | 17 |
| **KEEPING THE SPIRIT**<br>January 4, 1989 | 19 |
| **HEALING NATURE**<br>June 17, 1989 | 20 |
| **A BLOSSOMING TO A FULLNESS**<br>February 8, 1989 | 21 |
| **QUENCHING NATURE**<br>March 11, 1988 | 23 |
| **A PURE LIGHT**<br>August 23, 1989 | 24 |

| | |
|---|---|
| **ALL ALONE**<br>August 14. 1988 | 25 |
| **NATURE BRINGS JOY**<br>August 31, 1989 | 27 |
| **A THIN VEIL OF ETERNITY**<br>January 4,1990 | 28 |
| **TOUCH THE TREES**<br>February 2, 1990 | 30 |
| **TOUCH ME SAFE**<br>February 8, 1990 | 31 |
| **A CYCLE OF DESTRUCTION**<br>February 8, 1990 | 32 |
| **FORGIVENESS FINALLY COMES**<br>March 9, 1990 | 33 |
| **A RENEWAL**<br>February 9, 1990 | 34 |
| **HOW CAN I TRUST**<br>February 10, 1990 | 36 |
| **FREEDOM AT LAST**<br>February 16, 1990 | 39 |
| **TODAY**<br>November 21, 1991 | 41 |
| **HEALING TOUCH**<br>July 1991 | 43 |
| **AS I MEET MYSELF**<br>September 30, 1994 | 44 |
| **KAREN'S FRIENDS**<br>November 12, 1994 | 45 |
| **MY SMILE CAN'T HOLD MY TEARS ANY LONGER**<br>March. 18, 1995 | 51 |
| **POWER WITHIN A VICTIM NO MORE** | 54 |

| | |
|---|---:|
| **DADDY'S WEB**<br>September 3, 1993 | 59 |
| **BREAKING ENMESHMENT**<br>October 8, 1993 | 62 |
| **POWER**<br>July 27, 1993 | 64 |
| **SUNSHINE**<br>October 16, 1992 | 65 |
| **A VICTIM NO MORE**<br>July 31, 1993 | 66 |
| **WINGS OF FIRE**<br>October 15, 1992 | 67 |
| **PEELING THE OLD**<br>July 31, 1993 | 68 |
| **MORNING**<br>October 6, 1992 | 70 |
| **TEARS**<br>October 4, 1992 | 71 |
| **A CHILD GROWING**<br>August 13, 1993 | 72 |
| **WHOLENESS**<br>August 20, 1993 | 74 |
| **THE PEELING CONTINUES**<br>August 20, 1993 | 75 |
| **VICTORY**<br>August 6, 1993 | 76 |
| **A LOVE VICTORY**<br>August 10, 1993 | 77 |
| **A NEW LIFE**<br>July 27, 1993 | 78 |
| **POWER WITHIN**<br>August 1, 1993 | 80 |
| **A LOVE KEY — JESUS HOLDS IT**<br>August 1, 1993 | 81 |

| | |
|---|---|
| **IT IS JESUS!** <br> December 22, 1992 | 82 |
| **JESUS IS MY PEACE** <br> August 20, 1993 | 84 |
| **JIMMY, MY BELOVED** <br> November 1, 1993 | 85 |
| **MY HEART SWELLS WITH JOY** <br> January 29, 1994 | 86 |
| **RUSHING WATER** <br> September 30, 1994 | 87 |
| **REJOICE, OH MY SOUL** <br> March 9, 1995 | 88 |
| **MY SWEET, FATHER IN HEAVEN** <br> February 29, 1988 | 90 |
| **LIVING IN THE PRESENT** <br> February 25, 1996 | 91 |
| **PEACE AND UNREST** <br> March 17, 1996 | 94 |
| **A TRIBUTE TO MOM** <br> March 21, 1996 | 95 |
| **AN EAGLE** <br> April 28, 1996 | 96 |
| **EAGLES OF LIGHT** <br> April 28, 1996 | 97 |
| **EARTH LIFE** <br> May 25, 1996 | 99 |
| **MELODIES OF LIFE** <br> August 27, 1996 | 101 |
| **SUNSHINE LIKE THE SONSHINE** <br> May 16, 1995 | 102 |
| **UPON A HILL** <br> May 17, 1995 | 103 |
| **ME, AN INSTRUMENT OF PEACE** <br> May 18, 1995 | 105 |

| | |
|---|---:|
| **MORNING BECKONS**<br>June 9, 1995 | 107 |
| **CREATING ANEW**<br>June 9, 1995 | 108 |
| **I GO MY WAY**<br>June 18, 1995 | 109 |
| **A VEIL OF FOG**<br>January 25, 1997 | 111 |
| **MY FATHER**<br>December 6, 1997 | 112 |
| **LITTLE EAGLES**<br>February 22, 1999 | 113 |
| **ENJOY THE DAYLIGHT OF YOUR LIFE**<br>February 2, 1999 | 114 |
| **YOU DON'T HAVE TO WALK IN MY FOOTSTEPS**<br>February 2, 1999 | 116 |
| **SMILE**<br>August 6, 1987 | 117 |
| **BLENDING OF THE COLORS**<br>August 2, 1987 | 118 |
| **A GIFT OF THE SOUL**<br>September 7, 1987 | 119 |
| **CONCLUSION OF PART I**<br>THE JOURNEY OF AN EAGLE | 120 |
| **WIND FOR AN EAGLE**<br>May 14, 1999 | 121 |
| **PART II**<br>WHERE MERCY AND LOVE ABOUND | 123 |
| **ACROSS THE VEIL**<br>August 16, 2002 | 126 |
| **AN EAGLE SOARS**<br>July 24, 2002 | 128 |
| **MOM AND DAD LIVE**<br>July 23, 2002 | 129 |

| | |
|---|---|
| **COMFORT AND PEACE**<br>July 22, 2002 | 130 |
| **Listen To My Heart**<br>August 17, 2002 | 132 |
| **What's Your Hurry**<br>July 24, 2002 | 133 |
| **TAKE TIME**<br>July 24, 2002 | 134 |
| **JESUS SPEAKS TO MY HEART**<br>August 17, 2002 | 135 |
| **MY GOAL TO BE GENTLE AGAIN**<br>August 17, 2002 | 136 |
| **GOD HAS A PLAN FOR THEE**<br>August 17, 2002 | 137 |
| **CONCLUSION OF PART II**<br>Love and Mercy abound in the Righteous heart. | 138 |
| **ABOUT THE AUTHOR** | 139 |

# COMMENTS ABOUT THIS BOOK

**The Journey of an Eagle** is both **touching and inspiring.** My heart breaks for the child in you who endured suffering at the hands of others in such a violating manner. I admire you so much for the courage it takes to face the demons of the past and then share with others who have suffered so that they may be helped on their journey of healing.

This is **a remarkably personal and tender story** of betrayal and suffering by one who drew on her faith in God to write **a book that allows others drowning in pain to take this healing journey with her.**

*- Vick O.*

---

**"Journey of an Eagle,"** is likened to a tale of a young fledgling that grows and learns to fly, but while doing so, **it comes across trials and struggles to strengthen its wings.** Through the adversities of those struggles, the fledgling's wings are **strengthened by its faith in the Supreme Being** that gave it life and through this faith the young fledgling soars ever higher to stay on the path to become the great eagle it was destined for.

*- Michelle T.*

---

In reading **"Journey of an Eagle,"** I was so impressed with the **complete openness and honesty of the author** who tells of her life's experiences of abuse and incest. This is what everyone who has had this kind of experience **will greatly learn to heal from the inspirational truths** as well as be healed by the Lord through individual faith. What stands out is the parable of the eagle and the butterfly and what we can conceive from its teachings and incorporate it in our own lives.

*- Louise F.*

---

**The Journey of an Eagle** is a **book about healing and overcoming past hurt and pain**. The light is at the end of the tunnel and this book allows many of us to take a look at how the pain from our past can affect us in the future. The poems throughout the book **offer us an insight into the author's life**. It shows us the different stages of deliverance, the good and the bad, the chains and the release of the daily struggle that was held on to for many years.

This book is **heart breaking at times** but to read about how the Lord has set the author free **is encouraging and motivating.** This book has taught me that with the power of God every chain that bounds us will be released and we will become set free from past struggles, pain and hurt. The author gave us her heart in this book and it will **help other men and women who where abused seek freedom and joy through the power of Jesus Christ**. Amen

*- Kianna A.*

---

The "**Journey of an Eagle**" is a **heartfelt and emotional** description of one woman's painful but successful struggle to overcome the crippling shame of molestation. It is **a story of sorrow, redemption and joy** chronicled in storytelling fashion as well as poetry. One suffering from similar trials can find solace and inspiration in these pages.

*- Julie B.*

**The Journey of an Eagle was unexpected and breathtaking.** The author wrote with such emotion that made me think about some of my own suppressed memories that I too had to deal with at a point in my own life.

*- PJ G*

---

Your poems, and all the inspiration they carry, were read aloud with the company I had on Christmas Day, and **the Spirit was so moved** by them as to allow joyful tears flow in Grace!

*- Jeremiah*

---

**The Journey of an Eagle**

There are lots of Victims to molestation, some heal and others fall short. I hope this **book of short stores and inspiring poems** reach those who fall short and **help them heal, love and live whole lives**.

*- Karen P.*

# DEDICATION

This book is dedicated to my family; my parents, Donald Joseph Berard and Jeri Abb Lindsey; my siblings, Sharen Berard Keeler, Jerrie Berard Koroshes, Donald Joseph Berard Jr, Mary Jo Berard Adams, and Carl Berard; my husband, Jaime Efren Miño; my children, Daniel Patrick Twohy, Kenneth Michael Twohy, Katherine Zoila Miño, Karen Yolanda Miño Papagni, Mary Patricia Miño Estrada, Jamie Geralldine Miño Walsh; my grandchildren, Daniel Patrick Twohy Jr., Kristyn Marie Walker Twohy, Kymberli Dianne Twohy, Nicholas Cameron Twohy, Rex Twohy, Jade Twohy, Jordyn Alexander Miño, James Michael Branson, Sky Rose Branson, Izac Hunter Miño—Fox, Lily Suzanne Branson, Faith Katherine Branson, Isaiah Alvin Branson; my great-grandchildren, Milliano Papagni, Kymiyah Pratcher, Kydan Twohy, Kylee Twohy; and my future grandchildren.

We as a family can begin to have more peace in our hearts and treat others and ourselves as our heavenly Father's children. It begins with each of us, so we can have a more peaceful wonderful world to live in. Our lives can be more abundant and happy as we live the principles of the gospel that were taught to us by our Savior.

# PREFACE

The Journey of an Eagle is a Triumph story over the issues of molestation, emotional battery, emotional incest and verbal abuse. I created this book not only to heal me but to help others like me, to let them know that they aren't alone. Though the journey of recovery was difficult, it was worth everything that I devoted to the process of healing. I was given many teachers to help me heal. I received them with a grateful heart. Also, I want to say to the hurting soul, someone will be sent to help you. Ask and you shall receive.

I testify to you as a personal witness of recovery that there are rainbows after the storm clouds. You will be able to laugh again and be able to take control of your own life. It is possible. God will make it possible if you put your trust in Him. This place, earth, is a learning experience, a place to receive experiences for our own growth.

Sometimes I felt like there was no hope. Then God would send someone in my life to help me through another layer of life's garbage. By the way, garbage and stinky manure create beautiful flowers.

The Journey of an Eagle is actually a compilation of my other books, *Unsafe Touch to Healing Touch, As a Spirit Rises, Power Within,* and *a Victim No More.* I have made them into chapters in this completed book, The Journey of an Eagle. Even as I complete this work, the journey continues with many changes constantly at my door and life becomes a miracle in action.

As I write this chapter in my life, I was concerned about the timing of its existence. I was concerned that I would have to write my new chapter of this book. To my delight it was already written in my journals. "Thank you, Lord," was all I could say.

As I complete this book, I am a nanny. I take care of little eagles. They are so spirited and full of life. I learn constantly from them. I have learned the art of fantasy. I have learned the art of speaking truth as it is. I have learned to be more spontaneous. I have learned to be happier. I have learned that you can do many other things and still get the job done. For instance, I invited my five-year-old grandson, Jordyn, to clean the patio with me. He was three then. I took our portable tape player out on the patio and put a Beach Boys tape on. Well, the music played one of our favorite songs so we stopped what we were doing and danced. Then he hopped on his bike and rode around for awhile, while I hung clothes. Then we got the broom and swept leaves. Oh, Oh, another favorite song. So we dropped our brooms and danced and screamed for joy and wiggled our booties. It was so much fun. Then we went back to work, singing along with the music. We completed our work in a wonderful, joyous hour. I could have chosen to be a taskmaster. Instead, the work was done well and we had a great time laughing, dancing and playing.

I want to thank my many mentors and friends who have helped me on my journey. You have been a blessing in my life. God sees many of you to help me heal old wounds. He sent many of you just to have laughter in my life. He sent many of you as teachers. He sent many of you to teach me my self-worth. He sent many of you just to listen to all my crazy and wonderful ideas. He sent many of you to help me to find me. Thank you all for walking beside me even for a moment.

I thank my beloved husband for all his quiet support while I became an Eagle. I love him with all my being. His love radiates to me and to our family. His love quenches, repairs, heals, supports, caresses, and stabilizes my person —who I am.

I would like to thank my special angels who have been sent to help my whole body to heal. Douglas Canier and Ted Jones for body memory healing. Michael Carter and Robert DeMotte for my emotional healing.

I, most of all, want to thank Heavenly Father for allowing me to grow into the person that I am today. My gratitude can hardly be expressed in words for your faithfulness in my behalf. His love has been the key to my healing.

Thank you, Jesus, for your healing power and the plan of salvation. Thank you for choosing to be my Savior. I weep at all my sins, then I rejoice in the Atonement. I can't possibly thank you enough. This book is a small gift to you. I hope that the contents will uplift God's children and help them heal. I recognize that I could not have written this book without your watchful eye and the inspiration of the Holy Ghost.

## THE JOURNEY OF AN EAGLE

As I think of an Eagle, I see her flying alone attending to her business of soaring. Yet, I see her mingling with other friends to fulfill her journey.

In this section, The Journey of an Eagle is a collection of poems of more inner healing and gratefulness to my Lord and Master. It is a witness that He guided my journey. I am grateful to Him for all my healers, mentors, friends and adversaries during this period of growth.

May you enjoy my poems. May they bless your life. May you rejoice in God. Our Eternal Father and Jesus, Our Savior.

REJOICE IN EACH NEW DAY, is my prayer for you.

Karen Marie Berard Miño

## THE KITE AND THE HOLDER OF THE KITE THAT WE ARE

### January 12, 1998

A match made in heaven
I fly — He holds on
I flutter — He steadies the dance
I wander — He just plants himself
I come back to the arms of the holder

Then we dance again to fly the kite
I sway to and fro — He glides on the ground
I meet the birds — He meets the earth
We meet in harmony and love
As the kite is reeled in by the holder

The kite says — Let's fly!
The holder winces but dances anyway
He stays silent — the kite whirls and twirls
He knows danger — the kite just flies
Then a crackling sound awakens the holder
The kite has to be mended by the holder

The kite and the holder matched in heaven
To become destined to each other
The kite flies pleading with the holder
To dance and become one with her
Then we swing in peaceful harmony with the holder
As the kite is twirled into the arms of the holder

## **UNSAFE TOUCH TO HEALING TOUCH**

When I was about thirty-nine, I needed some answers about myself. Why did I constantly run away? Why did I scream and yell at my children? Why was I so frustrated with life? Why did I lock myself in my room? Why did I sit on my hands and cry and cry until I couldn't cry any longer? Why did I carry a smile and yet my soul was wallowing in tears? Why did I have a desire to be a hermit? Just WHY? WHY? WHY? I needed some answers quickly.

Here is my recovery story in a nutshell in this chapter. The latter part of the chapter is an accumulation of poems that were written during my healing process. They are my deepest feelings expressed in verse. They are the windows of my soul. I would lie in my bed staring at the ceiling for hours or even days with a cold blank stare, numb to the world around me. Sometimes I would go into our tiny bathroom and huddle in a corner sitting on the floor bathing myself in my uncontrollable tears. I would groan inside for help. *Someone, please, just help me,* I pleaded. Tormented! Why? I did not know.

My very own children annoyed me. Their squeaky little voices of demands haunted me. They echoed through the hallways of life. I couldn't shut them out for long for they tugged and pulled at my skirts. I just wanted to run away. Run away I did several times during their tender years. I needed to regroup my thoughts. What was causing such torture in my mind? I had so many voices, that I would put my hands to my ears and hope they would go away. I only wanted to hear one voice in my head. Then at times, I would contemplate dying. However, I would think about my beautiful large family. How would they survive without me, yet how would they survive with a mother so troubled?

I needed help now! Not tomorrow but NOW! I called my special friend from my kitchen. Sobbing and sobbing, I talked with him for hours and listened to his counsel.

"Can you help me?" I whimpered.

"Yes." He said. "When can you come?"

"I don't know. Let me see… How about next week? I'll give you a month, Michael. That's all I can arrange to stay away from my family," I sobbed.

"OK, let me know when you are in town," he said soothingly.

A short month to heal old wounds of yesterday. I had faith that Jesus Christ would help him to help me. I was packed in no time. I quickly organized my family. They were all cooperative. It made it so easy to leave. Kathy was in charge because Jimmy worked such long hours. She was the little mommy while I was away. Not only on this occasion but, on others. She was so responsible I trusted her implicitly. I don't know what I would have done without her. I needed this very special child. She is a valiant and great spirit. With my mind at ease, I proceeded to Seattle.

I stayed with Dorothy, a great and dear friend. She let Michael do the therapy sessions in her home. It was quiet and peaceful there like a calm lake on a Summer's eve. We were never interrupted. It made for real progress as we adventured into the past where secrets lie still.

During one session with Michael and Carol, I felt like an old piece of carpet drug through a war. Flu like symptoms were upon me, cold chills, spewing out the old dirt. Shivering, "I'm cold" I would say. So they covered me with a green velvet blanket. And yet, we continued with the past memories that were so deep, dark and hidden from me. The unsafe touch of molestation haunted me during my childhood and young adult life. I couldn't even give my children a bath after the age of five. I didn't feel comfortable. So, I didn't. I didn't know why. My inner-child, barely surviving, hid these memories away so I could deal with them now at the age of forty. A wise Move? I guess. However, I was a tormented soul constantly until I dealt with part of my past during these sessions. I felt that I was of no worth to anyone, especially myself and my family. As the bitterness unfolded, I became calm with the sweet aroma of forgiveness. Daylight was soon approaching. With a new rainbow over my head and the sun peeking out between the clouds, I could sing, write, dance and play again after a couple of weeks. An awful burden had been lifted from my soul within.

Then two years later, I needed more help. The Lord sent me another therapist. One thing I was taught that I have carried with me until now is this: Bob told me to see my past in this great big black and white picture and see my present and future in this tiny Technicolor picture in the corner. Then the miracle happened!

"Switch them," he said.

WOW!!! Yes, my present was here; my past is fading. Yes, just what I needed to learn. Now my hopes and dreams can come forth as I let go of the past. Today is today. I need to enjoy every minute. Yes, the past is past.

The process of refinement was starting. The Lord introduced me to others who helped me on my journey to find me. The Lord was purging my soul of iniquity step by step. It is a hard path. However, I am worthy of this great challenge of perfection. My greatest desire is to kneel once more at my Heavenly Father's feet and listen to His sweet, loving voice. Also, I can see myself throwing my arms around Him and saying, "I made it. It wasn't easy but you were there when I really needed you. Thanks, Father."

I must purify my life and pay attention to all that is around me. I must not live in a dream world anymore. The price is too high.

Now I feel like a new Spring day. Every day is a new experience. Now, no matter the circumstances that life affords, I rejoice in the everlasting gospel. Peace reigns in my soul.

Forgiveness is an important key to healing old wounds and new ones too. Forgiving yourself is the hardest thing to do. However, you must do this to heal. Forgiving others is essential also. The Holy Spirit will touch your spirit to forgive all the hurts in your life that are stunting your growth. If you listen to His small, quiet voice, you shall repair your life. Feel the Savior's healing touch as you align yourself with Him. It is a great miracle. It's like being washed and cleansed every whit from the inside out. I would liken it to an internal baptism. Then you shall be free to continue your journey on earth with peace in your heart.

I have written the following poems dealing with my emotions of healing. Step by step, the Lord has led me to victory. I praise Him and glorify Him. It is my desire to serve Him all the days of my life. Whatever He calls me to do, I will obey. He has been merciful unto me. As He purges my soul from iniquity, I rejoice in His healing touch.

Yes, the Savior's healing touch has pierced my soul. I humbly bow my head and give thanks to an Eternal Father who cares about me.

## JIMMY

DECEMBER 6, 1990

Jimmy, my sweet, sweet Jimmy
An anchor unto me
Patience set with gold

An example of worthiness
To our beloved children
A husband to emulate

My beautiful passionate, husband
I honor thee for all eternity
I thank God each day for thee

Jimmy, my sweet, sweet Jimmy
I love you beyond words
Thank you for loving me for me

## RUNNING AWAY
### September 25, 1990

Running away helped me to find me
Would it be good for you?
I can't say, but it was good for me

Now, can you run away and feel safe?
I could for I could meditate
And get away from all my cares

Sometimes though, I would have to face me
But there was always a special someone
To help and guide me through the rough parts

So running away helped me to find me
What about you? Can you run away?
I still can't say, but it was good for me.

## MOTHER HELP ME

SEPTEMBER 25, 1990

Mother help me
Enfold me in your strong arms
Embrace me
I'm sinking
Help me, Mother
Out of this pit
That I am in
You don't know that I'm there
Because I look strong
Give me your hand
Help me from me
So many voices inside
But yours would be so helpful
Please judge me not
Just put your arms around me.
Mother help me
Enfold me in your strong arms.

## A CHILD'S EYES

DECEMBER 23, 1988

A child's eyes say help me
And yet they can't read
Oh, help me, oh please help me
I am being hurt, I cry again.

Oh, please someone take courage
And save me from my loved ones
Who tells me that all is okay
And yet they violate me

Oh, that special someone came today
And saved me from these hurt souls
That have tormented me day and night
And now a peaceful slumber is mine

Thank you Lord, you heard me crying
And my soul wept for joy
Now, I can bloom and grow
And be what you want me to be

I know it won't be easy
Because my past keeps creeping up
But with all your tender help
I will become a pure angel again.

## **PROGRESSION**

DECEMBER 26, 1988

Progression halted
Overwhelmed by life
Deep despair enters in

Then new hope appears
A messenger is sent
To open doors again

A remembering of the past
Dealing with a tortured soul
Awaiting to be at peace

Then a sweet forgiveness
Is taught by the Master
To enrich a life so troubled

The gospel is taught again
Joy beyond belief
As blessings are pronounced

A great new beginning
For one who is whole again
To continue life's journey

Depression disappears
Walls are broken down
Progression continues

## LIGHT OVERCOMES DARKNESS

### JULY 14, 1999

It is dark so very dark
The mist of blackness thickens
I can't see any light

I cower all tight in a ball
Flooding my face with tears
Seeing no hope – no hope at all

Then a gentle hand reaches for me
And lifts me up to hug me
A friend, a really true friend

God sent her to wipe my tears
Just hold me, I whisper
Tell me it's going to be alright

Then another angel is sent
To help me heal the wounds of yesterday
And my tears fade away

As I pluck the darkness
One thing at a time
A little light enters in

Oh my, oh my
There's a rainbow standing by
Just to bring a smile to my face

Now, I can journey on
A little brighter, a little happier
Because I made room for God to enter in

## OLD HABITS ARE HARD TO BREAK
### December 28, 1988

Old habits are hard to break
Over and over again we repeat
The cycle of spiritual destruction

Take courage and trust in God
To teach you a new way
That will change you from night to day

Easy to say, I can give that up
Oh, not so easy to change evil ways
Persistence is the golden key

Don't give up on you
For you are worth saving
Take each step and go forward

As you progress willfully
Be diligent in your prayers
And keep God by your side

If you shall rebel
And get frustrated with life
Repent quickly to have Him near you again

We, working for perfection
Stumble and fall along the way
So get up and try again

Put a smile on your face
And hold the hand that will help you
To reach your final destination

With the Lord's help
You will be able to unlock
The door of all old habits.

## **VESSELS OF THE LORD**
DECEMBER 29, 1998

Oh, vessels of the lord
Listen, watch and pray
Be sensitive and caring
To those that are crying

Reach out and help
Take courage
And forget thyself
While doing His work

Rejoice on the dawn of each new day
As He gives you a chance to serve
His beloved and special children
And bring sunshine to their hearts

A new hope, is all they ask
Won't someone come and listen
To a heart so burdened with grief?
Come and be a light to such as these

The Lord will bless thee
As you reach and touch a soul
To lift a heavy burden
From a heart so distressed

Share the burdens of thy brother
So he may feel a lighter load
And then give all thy cares
To Him who will carry thee.

## KEEPING THE SPIRIT
### January 4, 1989

Listen to a very soft voice
A gentle voice of persuasion
As you do your daily chores

And He will whisper unto you
To help a special soul
That needs attention just from you

And your heart will rejoice with love
As you listen to this very soft voice
And partake of the gift of you

You will learn the Master's beauty
Of sharing, giving and receiving
When another soul will be touched by you

Joy will be yours, when you listen
To the gentle voice of persuasion
As you do your daily chores.

## **HEALING NATURE**

### June 17, 1989

To feel nature all around me
It gives me the energy to move
To feel the power of God within

As I sit quietly in my thoughts
I rejoice in God for His blessings
Especially the Gift of Nature

## A BLOSSOMING TO A FULLNESS
### February 8, 1989

Oh, how tight a bud I am
So afraid to open even a petal
Dare I take a peek into this new world
Will they ridicule and think me strange?

Then a voice said — take courage
And I will train thee in new things
So open a petal and feel abundant life
It is awaiting your timely arrival

Oh, how I love learning about me
God gave me a great inquiring mind
And so many wonderful talents
To share with all His children

Oh, Oh, they don't quite understand
And then I closed a petal or two
It's safe here — I'll withdraw
And they won't make fun anymore

Then I met someone, who cared
And taught again the gospel to me
And I rejoiced and progressed
And my petals began to fall forth

Then I knew my glorious worth
And my petals became full and rich
With the talents God gave unto me
To share with His other children

This time the color and fragrance — so sweet
That many accepted the gift of me
So I could give back to my Father
A blossom perfected in His love

I dare to be different and strange
In this new wonderful world
My petals open to share me
A tight bud in full bloom

## QUENCHING NATURE
### MARCH 11, 1988

In a hammock, I swing among the trees
The sun sends down its radiant beams
And the wind gently sways me
In communion with the Lord

The birds chirping overhead
To brighten such a heart as mine
As I swing, he teaches me
In the breeze, He quenches me

As the circle closes now
Nature heals my weary brow
Then the circle starts again
As I help another soul

As I continue to swing among the trees
The Son sends down His radiant beams
And the winds whisper unto me
A communion with the Lord.

## PRELUDE

I feel like God watches **over** me each day. He sends me messengers to help me through this life's journey. This following poem is a tribute to Him. I am so grateful for His light and enlightenment over my life.

## A PURE LIGHT

AUGUST 23, 1989

A pureness came over me
A light shined from within
Oh Behold! God can protect
With His life-saving Light!

Oh, ALLELUIA! ALLELUIA!
He is my Father
A protector of my spirit
To guide me in this life

A test, I must pass
So I can see Him once again
Be pure of mind and heart
And I shall see Him once more

I shall worship at His feet!
Sing ALLELUIAS to my Father
For His light has healed me
Pureness has come over me.

AMEN!

## ALL ALONE
### August 14, 1988

Alone I sit, pondering
And filling my soul
With all the beauties of nature

Close to home — this place
And yet a garden retreat
Just a few steps outside my door

Wind rushing through my hair
Refreshing my every limb
And cooling this tired soul

Alone, sometimes I need to be
To recapture my identity
And feel the voice of Eternal Peace

I belong to a very special one
Who watches day and night
To guide me to my Eternal home

I fall and fall every day
And yet I feel His presence
Picking me up along the way

All alone, I sit
Grateful for His gentle hand
That helped me to recommit

My life, I dedicate to Thee
Help me to serve Thee
Each and every precious day

## **NATURE BRINGS JOY**
### August 31, 1989

Nature brings joy to my soul
I breathe in all these wonders
And I feel refreshed inside

My soul sings to its music
And I rejoice in my Lord
My Father and Creator

All this wondrous beauty
Refreshes me inside
And brings joy to my soul

## A THIN VEIL OF ETERNITY
### January 4, 1990

A cloud mist hovering over the frosty grass
Like a veil between here and there
Only if I could reach through
And grab hold of every tomorrow

The road, would it be easier
If we could glimpse into our past home?
And see our lives as we were once before
So we could stay on that straight and narrow path

Who wants to give up Eternal Life?
But the flesh is so weak now
It battles with the spirit day after day
To gain pleasures of its kind

Spirit of mine, gain control
You only know what was before
And I, even in this flesh,
Know it is a sacred and holy place

I want to go back some day
In triumph and behold Father's face
And dance and twirl and rejoice
That I have made it home.

Life with all its trials
Overwhelms my soul
But I know it's Father's plan
To help me grow and grow

Be still my soul
Read, study and reflect
And rejoice in the Gospel plan
To carry me back home.

## **TOUCH THE TREES**

### February 2, 1990

As you stretch forth your arms
Feel the energy from the trees
These majestic wonders of the Creator
Give thee more life and force

They abound in the energy of life
To share if you take the time
To partake of such a wonderful gift
These creations of greatness and beauty

As the trees stretch forth their limbs
To cuddle you in their life force
Hold your hands up to them
And feel the gift of life go through you

Peace oh peace unto my soul
As I mingle among the trees
I learn to praise my Creator
As these trees do each hour of the day.

As I stretch forth my arms
I feel the energy of the trees
These majestic wonders of the Creator
Give me more life and force

STABILITY

## TOUCH ME SAFE
### February 8, 1990

What is this thing called touch?
Touch a spirit — touch a hand
Or touch a mind — touch a body
'Confusing' you say — can be sometimes

Who to touch — who not to touch
How do I discern this matter
Am I in a never-ending circle
Of no escape from unsafe touch?

There is help on the way
A plan is being made in your behalf
So reach out and be not afraid
To hold another's helping hand.

A hand that will create a safe touch
He will touch your spirit
He will touch your mind
You will be confused no more

## A CYCLE OF DESTRUCTION
### FEBRUARY 8, 1990

This cycle of destruction
Torments a weary soul

Rob virtue and give a gift
Confuses on soul

Give a Touch and get a gift
Oh that seems nice

But oh you see
It's all deceiving

A pattern has been set
To keep me off the track

A game — it's all a game
I learned to play very well

Survival is its name
And life is its end

Teach, oh teach me a new way
So life can be its fullest

## FORGIVENESS FINALLY COMES

### MARCH 9, 1990

Forgiveness has overcome me

And I shall go on and progress

Yesterday, a dream forgotten

To remember no more its sadness


I forgive thee, people of yester years

No more pain to grieve a tender soul

He has lifted me to newer heights

So I may continue my eternal journey


Thank you, my everlasting Brother

For atoning for the sins of mankind

your mercy has touched my spirit

I am grateful for the peace given to me.


AMEN! AMEN!

## **A RENEWAL**

### February 9, 1990

A renewed me is what I claim
To continue my path here on earth
To flourish as a blooming rose
So that I may serve my Creator

Love yourself — so you can love another
Is His plea with all mankind
Help each other without judgment
To reach your and their highest destiny

Love our Father first and above all
Worship Him with all your heart
So He can fill your soul with eternal love
To move you forward and progress as He did

He sends thee messengers
To help you along the golden path
Receive them with an open heart
So you can gain knowledge to endure

You can become like unto Him
One glorious step at a time
Be ye humble — so you may learn
All the lessons He has in store for you

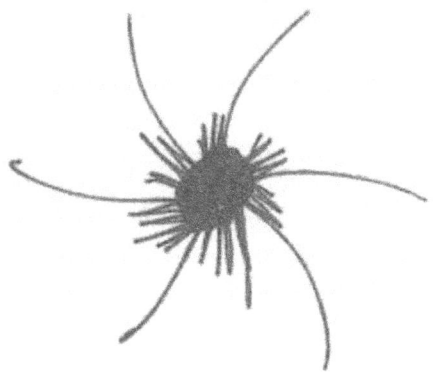

These growing opportunities are yours
To claim as a gift from the Lord
These blessings of life will help you
To reach your final destination

So accept your renewal in love
And go forth with His power and light
And teach another soul
What He has generously taught thee

## HOW CAN I TRUST
### FEBRUARY 10, 1990

How can I trust myself?
Will I make a wrong choice?
You left me helpless
Against this wicked world

Oh, this world would love to engulf me
It pronounces death unto me
And I speak life unto my soul
Through the power of the Lord

I know more than this world
So it has a partial impact
On my very vulnerable spirit
I will rise above this special hurt

You touched me wrong
I, a helpless child
Submitted unto wrongful desires
So keeping me a secret prisoner

I will escape some day
And be free from the torture
Of wrong discernment
You created for my life

The Lord is kind and just
You will get your reward
And 1 will be free
From the bond you set for me

He will send me help
So I can get on with living
Be productive and successful
In what I was created for

You stopped this creation
I hate you for this
Someday I'll forgive
I hope soon — So I can go on

My precious Father-in-Heaven
Has sent me a glorious man
To be my eternal partner
He has been an anchor unto me

He also has sent others
To aid me in this dilemma
I hope that I can trust
So I can be healed

A whole person is what I want to be
So I can be a powerful being of light
To help others who hurt like me
To become their destined selves

I can't take away their pain
Like mine — I have to struggle through
So shall they — but they will grow
Into a beautiful rose of life

Your soul will rest and be at peace
When I shall say, I forgive thee
And no more will I remember the pain
You caused unto my soul

I shall be victorious
And you shall bless me
And you shall bless God
For His tender mercy unto you.

## **FREEDOM AT LAST**
### FEBRUARY 16, 1990

Oh free at last
From the torment of evil
To love my companion
And to love God above all.

Free to make correct choices
No more double-mindedness
To set me off the tracks
And keep me from obeying

I rejoice in my Savior
His tender mercy has saved me
Alleluia, I give Him praise
My Lord and King forever

I now can go on
To make a new life for me
And my precious family
To be together for all eternity

Walls to break down
So all can be healed
From the torture of evil
That has overwhelmed us

As a family we can rejoice
In the everlasting gospel
Of love and sweet forgiveness
To unite us in our daily walk

The Lord is our Master
May we emulate His goodness
And share it with all mankind
For His honor and Glory.

AMEN!

## **TODAY**

November 21, 1991

Today closes its doors
As night brings twilight
And tomorrow comes again

Today forgotten
When not written down
A day to remember

Why Today?
It is all I have now
Today, This very day

Days whisk by
Unnoticed, Why?
A day is a day to hold

Are you having a good, joyous day
A sad tearful day?
Or an angry, mad day?

PEN WRITE!
For thoughts of today
Are tomorrow's dreams

Dreams come true
See it, speak it
Make it happen

Mirror an image
Value its being
Take time to notice

Today is your day
Live, just live
Make note of today

Tomorrows are
Of every today
Today is here – – – LIVE IT!

## HEALING TOUCH

### July 1991

Thou has cleansed my soul, O Lord
Thou has sent forth Thy hand
To touch a spirit that has wandered

Thou has sent forth thy light
To Illuminate my soul
With Thy everlasting wholeness

Savior Oh Savior of mine
Thank you for healing my heart and mind
With Thy healing touch of mercy

As I bend my knees to adore Thee
You fill my heart with thanksgiving
You have touched my weary soul

I felt Thy power
Like a rush of running water
Purifying my internal being

Thank you for your Healing Touch
That has made me whole again
To progress forward in eternity

## **AS I MEET MYSELF**
SEPTEMBER 30, 1994

As I meet me
I am unhappy
Because of my sinful ways
I cry, dear Lord
Save me from me
Help me to be more pure

As I meet me
I'm confused and not steadfast
Sometimes — I don't like me
Oh, dear Lord, help me
Your fallen child
Help me to be pure again

## PRELUDE

These friends of mine were emotional splits. I call them my friends because they protected me from all the hurt in my life. They could function while Karen, the core, could not. I feel God blessed me with them. However, I was tired of the many voices in my head. So in 1988, Michael and Carol helped me to integrate these emotional splits into me. I remember, while in a semi-conscious state talking to them individually, I let them know that we would become stronger if they would join me and become one. I had to convince them that they would not die. They finally agreed and I instantly became one. No more voices in my head. Oh, I was so grateful to God for sending Michael and Carol to my side at this time of recovery in my life.

My integration took place on March 2, 1988.

## KAREN'S FRIENDS

NOVEMBER 12, 1994

Katherine, oh dear Katherine
Born out of love for Karen
Bold and strong — Courage she had
Not to let people walk
Over the soft-spoken Karen

Katherine demanded perfection
She arose to the battle of right
Never would she back down
For losing was a loss to her soul
Winning a sure delight indeed

Oh Katherine, Oh Katherine
A battle of woes you conquered
Carried so many little ones
A Mother to all of Karen's friends
You became stronger and stronger

Katherine loved the Lord
Her bosom would fill with joy
As the choir would sing
"I believe in Christ"
"Yes," her reply, "I believe in Christ"

How can I be like unto Jesus
When I feel no gentleness
I will find gentleness, she thought
As she turned to think of Karen
She knew her gentle friend would help

Then Katherine introduced Debbie
Oh Debbie, How sweet she was
She loved to laugh and laugh
Born out of Karen's sorrow
To give her laughter each day

Karen would hear her laugh
This giddy-loud laugh
Contagious, you might say
It brought smiles to many frowns
And gaiety was in the air again

"If I laugh," Debbie would say
"It won't hurt so much
life could be cruel
and Karen needs me
to cheer her inner soul."

Then Katherine introduced Judy
Karen didn't like her much
Trouble was her game
And mischief she did cause
From time to time

Rebellion was her name
Conformity was not her plan
So Karen's friends helped to keep her still
Until Judy broke loose from their reign
And became a menace to those Karen loved

Then Karen's friends persuaded
Judy to repent of all her evil doing
Well that's OK until the next time
Then she'd creep into sinful ways again
To get the attention she needed to survive

Then Katherine introduced Janice
She was an open-hearted soul
Full of life and creativity
To bless the world around her
Especially Karen's little world

Janice was the creator of simple words
"Let's dance and play
So we can rejoice in loving
Like God wants us to,"
She would say each day

As the door closed on Karen's friends
They spoke softly to each other
To integrate and become a whole
To become one with their beloved Karen
To help her progress in this life

"Thank you, my friends"
Karen spoke unto them
"You have helped me to forget the pain
Now I remember when...
We must go unto better things.

You can help me still
You can be more powerful
You can be a warrior for Christ
You can be spirits full of love
You can be just like our Savior.

For now we will be one
As the Master touches our being
To be healed of all wrong doing
As He touches our inner-core
And cleanses our very soul

We will go forth as one
To bring souls unto Him
To bring celebration to life
So that He will be called blessed
As people watch our life.

INTEGRATION BECAME COMPLETE
MARCH 2, 1988

## MY SMILE CAN'T HOLD MY TEARS ANY LONGER

MARCH. 18, 1995

My tears are gathering in my eyes
Running down my cheeks
To put out my ever-present smile

Smile, Karen — SMILE
I tell myself — SMILE
You won't feel the pain if you just SMILE.
My smile can't hold my tears any longer

My tears are running away
Swiftly down my soak-filled chin
Oh my tears are running, running away
I can't hide the pain no more
That yester years have driven down deep in my soul

Yester years have driven down my emotions
Into a place so deep and dark
And now light is reaching my inner being

As the light reaches down into my soul
The darkness is drowning
With floods upon my face

I can't wash my face fast enough
My eyes are swollen with memories
A flood of tears is drowning my face

Tears, tears of yester years
Just swell out and heal
So I can live my life with awareness

I can be as good as I want to be
Not like daddy wants me to be
But like God wants me to be

God wants you to accept all of you
The very good and humble you
And the very evil and prideful you

You say when you look at your children
You see yourself staring at the mirrors
You want to run away — you say

Your mirrors are good and bad
Just not bad, you see
Good also reigns in all your little mirrors

Gentleness and kindness
Reigns in the hearts of your mirrors
So look at them and rejoice

Profanity and anger
Stirs your heart to dance
Mirrors of ugliness that can change

Karen, your mirrors are your teachers
They will help you see you
Accept you. Karen, accept you

When you accept you, Karen
The tears will be drier
So you can smile again

Then the sun will appear
The rainbow will come
And your tears
Will only trickle on your smile

Your smile will then heal not hide
The wounds of yesterday
Your tears will cleanse them
And your Savior will remove them

## **POWER WITHIN A VICTIM NO MORE**

This chapter deals with my healing journey with the Savior and the messengers who were sent to me. I feel that each of us has to find our own path home to our Creator. There are easier paths than others. However, we are taught in the scriptures that the path is narrow to our heavenly home.

When I wrote "Unsafe Touch to Healing Touch," I thought that it was the end of my writings concerning this subject. However, as I live each new day, I realize that it was only the beginning of a new walk, a new power within, and a new release of shame of yester years.

Life is about choices. As life continues, I realize that I need to really listen to my inner voice so that I don't make destructive choices concerning my spiritual growth. Though I may make wrong choices for myself, I have decided in my life to repent quickly and learn from these experiences. Also, I choose not to beat myself forever for making a mistake. There is solace in the atonement of Our Savior, Jesus Christ. Without His sweet mercy, I don't know if I could survive the rest of my life.

The natural man in me wishes to taste all the pleasures of life, yet, the spiritual man in me wishes to choose control over the flesh. Sometimes I feel like I am on the battlefield ~ the Natural Man versus the Spiritual Man. My spirit man reaches for the higher power within me and seeks forgiveness and mercy from the Lord. I will be victorious and my spirit shall rule over my body.

There is hope in Christ. We have a Savior. My soul sings alleluias because of my belief in Jesus, my friend, Savior and my Lord. He makes it possible to have my scarlet self turn into a brilliant white. So when I see Him someday, I can kneel and adore Him at His throne. I can kiss His feet and receive mercy for all my sins. I need to rejoice in His atonement and receive power within to share His goodness.

A friend shared with me an idea that I would like to share with you because it has made an impact on my life. Pretend that you are going to die on Saturday. You have a date with the Savior. How are you going to prepare to see Him? Live each day as though you have a date with the Savior on Saturday. For surely, your Saturday will come sooner or later.

Now, the power to move ahead with my life comes from Jesus. He has helped me become new. I feel powerful. I need this new power to do my life's work. My work is to share with you, my friends, that there is hope in Christ. No matter what pit we or someone else dug for us, we can recover. Take the hand of a friend and rely on the arm of Jesus. There were many people in my life sent by God to help me through my recovery. They gave me new keys to continue my life with purpose and thanksgiving. I also feel that recovery is a continuous process. A process of peeling the old and accepting the new. A brilliant vibrant and new me is always a continuing journey. Life is about progression.

Before I started the sessions with Douglas, I attended an Emotional Incest Seminar. It dealt with the daddy's little girl syndrome. Oh, how painful it was to see my whole life radiate around this enmeshment. My choice of friends, my choice of husbands and my choices in general were governed by this enmeshment of daddy and me. It left me crippled to make wise choices in my relationships as well as my life's work.

As I am going through the twelve-step program of a Spiritual Journey, the pain of enmeshment is almost unbearable. It is a crippling disease. As I share my feelings of unworthiness and isolation, I cry bitterly. However, there is a power within that is helping me cope. It is helping me make new choices. It is helping me serve without being co-dependent. It helps me have new boundaries with my friends, husband, children, and grandchildren. It is a step-by-step process.

I am beginning to appreciate ME — And — OH YES ~ Success is becoming a warm blanket around me. I have new joy in each new little success of my life. Thanks to Jesus and all His servants (that's you, all my friends) for helping me be the best ME.

I would like to share a session of healing with you. It took place on my seventh session of deep tissue integration with Douglas. As he was working on my neck, I cried out, "I hate you, I hate you! You robbed me of my innocence, I hate you!"

Then I cried and cried. This was the first time that I have cried about my molestation when I was seven years old. Douglas just placed his hands on my head and shoulders and said nothing. He let me vent my anger and distress. Then I said out loud, "I AM NOT A VICTIM ANYMORE, I RELEASE YOU FROM MY LIFE. YOU CAN REST NOW, FOR I WON'T CARRY YOU AROUND WITH ME ANY LONGER!" It was a turning point in my life.

The following week, we continued with the seventh session. Because I could not do any more work that day, he finished my session with a nurturing massage. When we continued the work, the real nurturing and miracle took place. Something inside gave up the victim – – ME. I wanted to shout to the world "I AM NOT A VICTIM ANYMORE, AND I HAVE POWER WITHIN!"

# I AM NOT A VICTIM,
# I AM NOT A VICTIM,
## I AM NOT A VICTIM,
## I AM NOT A VICTIM,
### I AM NOT A VICTIM,
#### I AM NOT A VICTIM,

# I AM FREE.

I AM FREE TO MAKE NEW CHOICES. I AM FREE TO SAY NO! I made a deal with the Lord. I asked Him to let me know if I am in a dangerous situation – *Please – don't whisper – yell in my ear, Lord, so I can hear and act without fear,* was my plea. *Please yell in my ear – so I won't freeze and be a victim again.* So, he has kept His promise. He yells in my ear so I can hear – so I can get away from danger. Thank you, Jesus, now I can truly say NO and a VICTIM NO MORE.

As I contemplate this new energy of life, I wonder if I can share it, control it, and create with it. The answer is "YES! Karen, you can." With my new awakened life force, I can use my talents to the fullest. I can draw, dance, write, sing, play and whatever God has given me as a talent. Maybe I can explore new talents and develop them. Maybe I can use my energy to serve God's people.

I can live in the NOW, not in yesterday – BUT NOW! I can live each day to the fullest and have JOY NOW! Joy – A peace of mind and of spirit – That is how I would define Joy.

I rejoice in my new life! I thank my Heavenly Father for the Gospel of Jesus Christ. I feel free to do my life's work. I feel alive! I feel my whole person being awakened from a long sleep. I'm glad this has happened to me now while I'm still here on earth. I'm grateful to myself for the courage it has taken to get here.

The following poems are about my new power within. Peeling off the old me and gaining the new me. I will be victorious with Jesus at my side —

ALLELUIA!

## Many Alleluias
## Amen & Amen
## My victory Poems:

## PRELUDE

My father and I were close — too close. I followed him everywhere when I was little. Hands in his pocket, hands in my pockets. I went with him to Mass every morning at 5:30 A. M. to the convent. He was their altar boy, helping the priest.

I loved my daddy so much. However, my family used my relationship with my father to their benefit. "Karen," they would say, "go ask daddy if we can go here or go there." It left me enmeshed with my father.

When he died, a part of me went into the grave. Now, I would have to stand alone. How scary was that? Very scary. He died on April 20, 1978. Now my journey of healing was just starting. The torment of voices, the running away, the emotional outbursts, all started to happen.

Why? Because my daddy left me.

## DADDY'S WEB

SEPTEMBER 3, 1993

Daddy, daddy
Your little girl
Possessed by you
Intertwined by emotions

Daddy's web
Can I come with you?
A little shadow
Following Daddy everywhere

Daddy's Web
Closing tighter
Can't get away
I'm Choking

Daddy, Daddy
I want to be free
Went away to school
I can breathe a little bit

Daddy's Web
Creating enmeshment
Intertwining of friendships
Made so intense.

Daddy, Daddy
Free me, is my plea
Release the hold
That followed you to the grave

Daddy's Web
Creating jealousies
That seem so unfair
Broken hearts—theirs and mine

Daddy, Daddy
Don't you know
They all used me
For their own pleasure

Daddy's Web
Creating unsafe touch
Touch of Emotions
Touch of enmeshment

Daddy, Daddy
Heal yourself
It's OK to stand alone
Be brave, you have the courage

Daddy's Web
I break this very day
So I can grow and grow
And be the Woman that I am

Daddy, Daddy
Hear my plea
Release me from your web
So I too can stand alone.

## **BREAKING ENMESHMENT**

OCTOBER 8, 1993

Set me free from enmeshment
Then I will clearly breathe
I will stand safely
No more will I wish for another
Because you set me free

FREE? You ask
YES! FREE!
Free of imprisonment
Free of jealousy
Free to make friends

Release me of your stronghold
Let me be my true self
So I can love you even more
Grow to your destiny
Cling not to mine

We may share destinies
We may walk side by side
We may continue progressing
We may hold each other
We may dance the same steps

However, each has his own way to travel
Each has his own mission to fulfill
Each has his own talents to share
Each has his own love to give
Each has his own life to answer for

Honey, be brave this day
Take courage in Jesus
He will lead you each day
To His people who need you
You are a precious gift

As we grow together
We can grow separately
So we each can be whole
So we each can give a gift

As we walk hand in hand
Jesus will be at the fore front
He leads our eternal path
To the glory that we were created for
Eternal life — Man and Wife together

## **POWER**

July 27, 1993

CREATE POWER WITHIN
Listen to the quiet voice
Act upon your guidance
Don't delay — Don't ask why
Just act — He knows danger
Listen, Act, Rejoice!

RECEIVE POWER WITHIN
Rejoice in the Spirit!
Dance to the tunes of today
Rejoice in Life!
Accept life and its abundance
Give glory to our Creator of life
He gives us power
Receive it from Him
Who giveth liberally
Listen, act, rejoice!

RECEIVE POWER WITHIN

## SUNSHINE

October 16, 1992

SPREAD SUNSHINE

INSTEAD OF VAPOR BLACK

SMILE! SMILE! SMILE!

TURN YOUR HEART A SWIRL

## A VICTIM NO MORE
### July 31, 1993

Now choices are clearer

I say to myself — VICTIM NO MORE

Eyes are opening — Shame leaving

A VICTIM NO MORE, I say


You have no power — shame

I release you from my life

Like a tree with crumbled leaves

Falling as the wind blows


VICTIM, NO MORE, I say

Plucking bad thoughts of yester years

As a tree needs help to prune

The old leaves of yesterday


VICTIM NO MORE, I say

New life like a tree in spring is mine

A radiant full life to behold

To continue Victorious with new choices

## WINGS OF FIRE

### October 15, 1992

STRENGTH

Wings of fire
Gliding mysteries
Through timeless space
Connecting emotions

Rain on smoldered trees
Quenching tired brows
Mist of showers
Surrounding the world of pain

Sunshine faces
Peaking through the gates
Smiling on the windows
That heart penetrate

## PRELUDE

I feel like my journey of healing was like the Autumn

When leaves drop to the ground

And like the Spring

When new leaves return with new life.

## **PEELING THE OLD**

July 31, 1993

Crumbled leaves of yesterday

Shedding the Body's memories

So new life can continue

With Hope and Love together

Oh, memories of old

Clinging to this Natural Body

Be plucked from the core

So new life can continue

Bring the New Green Life

In its fullest Glory

So the wind can carry the old away

Far away from the Heart Path

Peeling the old memories
is painful and joyful
Simultaneous growth of Newness
Dance over the crumbled leaves

Hear them crackle under your feet
See how they enmesh in the earth
Where does the old leave and the new begin?
See! The New Life is radiant

*TRANSITION*

New Life, like a rainbow
after a tropical rainstorm
New Life, like a sunbeam of morning
Glowing through the darkness of night

New life coming to you
Swirling in the sunbeams
Over the new vibrant trees
Crumbling the leaves of yesterday

## MORNING

October 6, 1992

As I awaken — I stretch to feel
The cool brisk air of Morning
Settling on my brow

Morning air — the freshest
Like a. crisp red Washington apple
Stored in a cool dark cellar

Morning —- A peaceful time
A renewal of energy
A time to meet new challenges

Morning — Full of confidence
To heal all old wounds
That stagnate and reinfest

I praise God for the Morning
The golden sunrise
A promise of today

Heavenly Father

Birds chirp and chatter
At the very break of day
To awaken all with a song

Morning — A new beginning
To renew all covenants
To follow the Golden Path

## **TEARS**

OCTOBER 4, 1992

A tear trickling down a cheek
To wet a bosom full of sorrow
For the sins of my own pressed soul

Repentance is the only key
To unlock the hard door of this heart
That has fallen into sinful ways

A key, the Savior says, I give unto you
To unlatch such a mournful heart
So you may enter unto my peace

Then shall the tear trickling down
Turn to sobs of joyful forgiving
As the Savior extends His mercy on my soul

## PRELUDE

I sucked my thumb until I was thirteen. However, when I started my journey to heal, I started to suck my thumb again. When I felt lonely and abandoned, I would crawl into my bed, cover myself up and put my pillowcase to my nose and suck my thumb. I would tell myself that everything would be okay now, Karen

## A CHILD GROWING

### AUGUST 13, 1993

As I suck my thumb
I remember the cozy feeling of the womb
Embraced by my Mother's warmth
A sanctuary while growing life

As I suck my thumb
I remember the quiet feeling
Growing a head, a leg, an arm
and all my parts in harmony

As I suck my thumb
I remember my Heavenly Home
The friends that I left behind
and the friends that I have found here

As I suck my thumb
I remember the tender moments
Of my Mother's breast leaning next to me
Cuddling my head in her gentle arms

As I suck my thumb
I remember a growing child
A child in her teens unwanted
Trying to make her own path

As I suck my thumb
I regain my strength to grow
My inner child healing
From all the wounds of yesterday

As I suck my thumb
I ponder childhood play
I want to do that again
Play as an innocent child

As I suck my thumb
Trying not to feel the danger
Of a growing child in an adult body
Oh – it scares me so

As I suck my thumb
I grow and grow
It's going to happen
I will be a grown child soon

As I suck my thumb
The pain of growing overcomes me
And I am jubilant to find
That I have reached my destiny

As I suck my thumb
I am secure in my Mother's womb
Growing Life ~ A growing child
TO COME FORTH AND BE ME!

## **WHOLENESS**
### August 20, 1993

Complete wholeness
I feel — this very day
As I ponder yesterday

No Matter — Yesterday
It is Today that counts
This very moment — Today

Today — I am complete
I feel Wholeness
A new life to behold!

As I ponder yesterday
It is healed by forgiveness
I do forgive me and others

As I walk today
I have the power to be me
I have the power to love all men

That is me
A loving light of Christ
A vessel of life renewed

Complete Wholeness
is what I feel today
As I ponder yesterday

## THE PEELING CONTINUES

### August 20, 1993

The peeling continues
The stripping of pain

Replaced by smiles
Replaced by laughter

The peeling continues
Memories washed by tears

Replaced by peace
Replaced by inner solitude

The peeling continues
Soaked in the Lamb's blood

Replaced by rejoicing
Replaced by power within

The peeling continues
A Victim no more

Replaced by forgiveness
Replaced by eternal love

## VICTORY

August 6, 1993

Every day a new victory
A walk in the light path
Blessing all the children of man
With each hello and smile

Walking the victory
Kneeling and asking for guidance
to protect each thought and action
So self can be honored

Oh, listen to the core
So the victory may remain
Each day that you live
Until the final day of mortality

Then victory will be yours
As you meet the Savior
and walk with Him
Back to your Heavenly Home

## A LOVE VICTORY

AUGUST 10, 1993

I AM ACCEPTED
I AM ME
GOD DOES LOVE ME
IT IS A L OVE VICTORY

I feel clean again
I feel white as snow
Jesus did this for me
It was a LOVE VICTORY

I AM ME
A WHOLE AND NEW ME
HEALED FROM WITHIN
IT IS A LOVE VICTORY

A Love Victory
A Love Victory
Jesus has healed me
A LOVE VICTORY

I AM A VICTOR
I AM NOT A VICTIM
I AM NOW ME
IT IS A LOVE VICTORY

## A NEW LIFE
### JULY 27, 1993

See a tree full of life energy.
Some green and old Spots need to be pulled.
Then Green comes in the fullest.
A new abundance of life is created.
All new life is here!

A new you is born.
Peel away the old yesterday memories
and let them fall.
Then pluck the old habits of shame and guilt
So you can live full and prosperous

Sorrow and guilt for sin are okay
As long as you use them
to change your life into newness.
A renewed commitment to serve God!

Oh Jesus, thank you for your atonement.
It gives me strength and peace.
It cleanses my soul.
I rejoice!

I am sad for a while about the nail
That I helped push into your hand.
Then, I remember the resurrection unto life
I rejoice and dance in jubilation!

Thank you for your mercy, my Savior.
Forgive me, your servant, for the wrong choices.
The flesh is so weak.
My spirit is strong.

Now I need to make the flesh strong,
Healthy and pure!
Make the flesh like the green tree.
It, like the tree

I will have abundant life
As the old peels away.
The new life is here
Partake of it TODAY!

## **POWER WITHIN**
### August 1, 1993

I receive power for me
To live an abundant and full life
A life with love and healing
Jesus helps me to have this Power

A cleansing Power washes me
Like the trickling rain washes the earth
A power that lives within
Helping me with choices to make

Power to come forth
Telling the work of God's goodness
Speaking truth to all who will listen
And obey His gentle ways of gold

Power to love comes from within
He surrounds me with His glory
To share with others ~ His mercy
A Power I receive for me

## A LOVE KEY – JESUS HOLDS IT
### AUGUST 1, 1993

As I kneel myself before the Lord
I beg for mercy for sins committed
I plead with Him
To forgive me for my sinful ways

Oh, Lord forgive me, my flesh is weak
My spirit wishes to obey ~ and then I fall
Oh flesh of mine, listen to the voice inside
And commit no more sins that blacken my soul

Repent ye, repent ye, the prophets say
The Blood of the Lamb
can wash my scarlet self
into a being of brilliant white

As I kneel myself before the Lord
His hand is felt upon my head
My daughter, sin no more
Thou art forgiven from all thy sins

## IT IS JESUS!

DECEMBER 22, 1992

Through the darkness
Through the darkness
Through the darkness

    IT IS JESUS
    IT IS JESUS

Through the shadows
Through the shadows
Through the shadows

    IT IS JESUS
    IT IS JESUS

    I see a light
    I see a light
    I see a light

    IT IS JESUS!
    IT IS JESUS!

He wraps His arms around me
He wraps His arms around me
He wraps His arms around me

    HE IS JESUS
    HE IS JESUS

    His light engulfs me
    His light engulfs me
    His light engulfs me

HE IS JESUS!
HE IS JESUS!

His love penetrates my soul
His love penetrates my soul
His love penetrates my soul

IT IS JESUS
IT IS JESUS

I walk with my friend
I walk with my friend
I walk with my friend

HE IS JESUS
HE IS JESUS

I bask in His light, like the sun's rays
I bask in His light, like the sun's rays
I bask in His light, like the sun's rays

HE IS JESUS
HE IS JESUS

AMEN! AMEN! AMEN!

## JESUS IS MY PEACE
### August 20, 1993

Jesus is my Peace
As I walk in His light
He radiates His peace

It feels like sunshine
Pouring down on a Spring day
Basking in His love

Inner Peace — a quiet
A solitude of voices
Now one reigns within

Thank you, Jesus
You are healing me
From memories of yesterday

My body is at Peace
Fire is flickering
Light is remaining

My emotions are calm
Like a lake on a hot day
Soothed by the water therein

My Spiritual Self
Enlightened by the light
That reigns over eternity

Jesus is my Peace
His light radiates my soul
As I walk in His Peace

## JIMMY, MY BELOVED
### November 1, 1993

BEHOLD, A DREAM!

IT'S YOU! IT'S YOU!

Holding my hand forever

Embracing me with your arms

Covering line with your kindness

Counseling me with your wisdom

Dancing with me cheek-to-cheek

Talking with me for hours and hours

Working beside me

Growing together for Eternity

## MY HEART SWELLS WITH JOY
### JANUARY 29, 1994

My heart swells with joy
And I wonder about eternity
I get scared sometimes
What does life Matter?
And then I get the answer
You matter and what you do
People are blessed by you
By your smile, and giving way
They trust and honor you
Karen, be calm and quiet
Listen to your inner-self
It will lead you on the Path
The Path of Golden Rainbows
The Path of Silver Chimes
As you walk daily with God
Karen, listen and obey your heart
Surround yourself with goodness
Protect your Spirit with good uplifting things
Let not your mind wander into dark paths
Search and search for the light
The light of Jesus will guide you home

## RUSHING WATER
### September 30, 1994

Rushing water
Cleanse my very soul

Rushing water
Run to my inner core

Rushing water
Whisk over my body

Rushing water
Cleanse me from head to toe

Rushing water
Whisper clean thoughts in my ears

Rushing water
Bring me to Celestial Shores

Rushing water
Purify my stubborn heart

Rushing water
Fill me with your strength

Rushing water
Cleanse my very soul

## **REJOICE, OH MY SOUL**
### MARCH 9, 1995

Rejoice, oh my soul
For I sing praises unto God
To lift my heart from sorrow

Rejoice, Oh my soul
For He walks with thee
Until the sun lays to rest

Rejoice, Oh my soul
He comforts you
When your shoulders are heavy with grief

Rejoice, Oh my soul
He gives thee wisdom
When your speech is from the heart

Rejoice, oh my soul
He laughs with you
When you play in the grassy fields

Rejoice, oh my soul
The Savior has come to your home
To dwell and partake of goodness

Rejoice, oh my soul
For the atonement of Jesus
Who cares so much for me

Rejoice, Oh my soul
Be light and merry of heart
And stay on the light path

Rejoice oh, my soul
The Savior has given us keys
To open the wounded heart to heal

Rejoice, oh my soul
For the blessings untold
That I receiveth every hour

Rejoice, oh my soul
Be happy and sing praises
To the Father and the Son

KAREN MARIE BERARD MIÑO

## **MY SWEET, FATHER IN HEAVEN**
### FEBRUARY 29, 1988

Feeling free as a child
To commune with my Father
Pureness and innocence abide
When I am in His presence.

Light surrounds us
Glowing all around
The throne of Our Father
In our Celestial Home

He makes me feel welcome
As I approach His throne
Arms waiting to receive me
And comfort me at last.

Just to be in His presence
Quiets my whole soul
Everything is peaceful now
As I rest in His bosom

I crave to be near my Father
So I must pray more often
To be close to Him in Spirit
And feel of His divine nature

Peace be unto me
As I commune in prayer
To my Eternal Father
Who is in Heaven

Amen

## PRELUDE

As I was doing the spiritual journey group sessions at St. Luke's church, I became aware that I was living in the past, wishing for the future. So, then, I woke up and started to live in the present. It was exciting. I started to enjoy my life's journey as it came. Also, I didn't fight against it so much. Life was tasting better and better like a piece of cheesecake with cherries dripping down the side.

## LIVING IN THE PRESENT

### FEBRUARY 25, 1996

As I ponder living in the present

I think of my pre-mortal existence
I think of my earthly past
I think of my near future
I think of my distant future

Then I wake up and say, all I have is today

I have today to smell the fragrance of nature
I have today to say I love you
I have today to give hugs and kisses
I have today to pray to God above

I have the present to feel the Sunshine in my life

I have today to be grateful for the Gospel
I have today to be with my loved ones
I have today to be reverent in nature
I have today to be thoughtful towards others

I have the present to feel the rain in my life

I have today to feel the sorrow for my sins
I have today to repent from my wrongdoings
I have today to remove obstacles that keep me from Jesus
I have today to cry for what I feel inside my heart

I have the present to see the rainbows of God

I have today to count all my blessings
I have today to see God in nature
I have today to paint, write, dance, play, serve
I have today to sing, rest, compose, read and study

I have the present to know the Savior more

I have today to read the scriptures
I have today to walk with another
I have today to smile and give sunshine
I have today to pray and sing

I have the present to sing alleluias to God

I have today to shout praises to my King
I have today to rejoice in the journey of life
I have today to sing from the depths of my soul
I have today to dance before the Lord of Lords

As I ponder the present and living to the fullest

    I often think of pre-mortal existence
    I often think of my earthly past
    I often think of my near future
    I often think of my distant future

Then, I wake up and say all I have is Today

    I have today to do all God requires of me
    I have today to be glorious in my countenance
    I have today to say a kind word
    I have today to worship my God and King

            AMEN

## **PEACE AND UNREST**

### MARCH 17, 1996

Peace in my heart
As my spirit shines forth
I know who I am
Yes, I am a child of God
A daughter of royalty

Talents, I behold many
I can dance, sing, direct choirs
Play, compose music, teach, write, garden
Nurture plants and children and the elderly

I can bless many with my smile and my laughter
And yet, when someone does me wrong
I can't partake of their nature
I can't embrace them

Oh, My Savior, teach me
Teach me to be like you
How can I hug any one?
Heart of mine, stop and behave
How can people feel okay?

Be like a little child, the Master said
So I watch
They forgive, they see no guile
Do they not see our inhumanity?

Tears welling up in my eyes
Oh, Lord teach me to be like one of them
So I can stand with no guilt

## A TRIBUTE TO MOM
### March 21, 1996

The Lord knows a woman
I name her Mother

As a child

She rocked me, cradled me and sang to me
She danced with me and taught me
She bathed me, fed me and worked with me

The Lord teaches this woman
I still call her Mother

As I grew

She prayed with me until my heart was full of joy
She loved Jesus, You could tell as she wiped a tear
She acted with purpose, as she visited the afflicted

The Lord molds this woman
I today call her Mom

As I became older

She'd hug and dance with me
She'd laugh until the wee hours of morning
She'd whisper, thank you dear Lord for my family

The Lord knows this woman
I named her mother

As I am grown

She walks, laughs and dances with me
She visits, cheers up and smiles with the afflicted with me
She prays, talks and shares her life with me

## AN EAGLE

April 28, 1996

An Eagle in waiting
Feed her — Nourish her
Taunt her — Play with her
Teach her ~ Mingle with her
Love her — Put your arms around her

## PRELUDE

As I journey on earth, I notice that even when we become eagles, we can become hurt and broken. It takes other eagles to mend us and care for us. Sometimes, it just takes other eagles to pray for us. So, I ask for their prayers and help, when I am broken in spirit. They come and help. Also, I go to other eagles and help them. It is a circle of love that we create for each other.

## EAGLES OF LIGHT

April 28, 1996

They, God's children, helped me
Be an Eagle of Light
As I glide through the air of life
I say, thank you to my friends


When a wing is broken
Others aid in healing
Encouraging, you'll fly again
They pat and sow the wings


Then they take me to a mountain
"See -- you can fly like us
Stretch forth your wings"
Then a miracle -— I fly

The other Eagles fly around
Dip and glide and soar with glee
They wave good-bye
And leave me alone to soar

Then I prepare to mend other Eagles
I pat them and Sow them
I kiss and embrace them
So they can also soar to heaven

Then I take them to the mountains
And show them — they can fly also
"Come ~ set on my tail
Now fly and whirl and glide"

Then I wave — good-bye
"I'll see you around my friends
Now is your time to soar alone"
And help another Eagle mend

Now as I glide through life
I meet all my eagle friends
We are all Eagles of Light
We are God's children

## EARTH LIFE

MAY 25, 1996

Who do I touch living here on earth?
My existence — Is it worth it?
Do I act with noble character?
Can I learn more about me as I journey here?

I hear the cries of earth to God
"Oh release me from these wicked people
When will it end, Lord?
When will you cleanse me from evil?"

These cries of the Earth are mine also
"Oh, Lord when will you release me?
Oh, Lord help me not to fall into evil ways
Oh, Lord help surround me with holy people."

The answer — Comes distinctly
"My daughter, My time is not your time.
There are things to learn and study
You have important work to do."

Karen, cleanse your mind
Smell the fragrance of your garden
Prioritize all your time on earth
Have joy and happiness doing your choices

Sing, Karen, Sing praises to God
Rejoice, your soul, Rejoice in this day
Let not a day slip by — To feel all
Pray, Karen — So the tempter may not tempt thee.

You shall touch many souls
Awake, listen to the still small voice within
Your existence is worth more than gold
As your journey here on earth to find you.

## MELODIES OF LIFE
### August 27, 1996

As I walk along the Path of Life
My heartbeats at a regular beat
Then when I meet someone sweet
My heart dances to a different beat

And when I meditate
My heart slows to a softer beat
So I can rejuvenate myself
And be on my merry way

Life is a melody of music
Dramatic though it may be
It stimulates the soul
To move in all directions

My life has to be full
So I feel so complete
Each day — A new experience
So I can learn and be all I can

As I walk the Path of Life
My heart beats up and down
A melody it creates
As I walk here awhile

## SUNSHINE LIKE THE SONSHINE
MAY 16, 1995

Sunshine basking on my whole being
Giving me warmth and light
That I need for the journey called life

Yet without the Sonshine
I would be a vessel of darkness
Roaming the earth with no purpose

He gives me a reason for life
Life in abundance to share
He lifts me when weary and confused

He rescues me when I depart His ways
He just loves me and comforts me
How do I deserve such a companion as He?

Thank you, Jesus, you give me hope
Hope to continue life with purpose
Hope to live so I may live forever

Hope to see you again
Hope to see my father and mother again
Hope to have my family with me

Hope because of your atonement
Hope to live life through eternity
Hope to have my husband at my side

Thank you again, My Master and Savior
For teaching me your ways
So I may have sunshine in my life

## UPON A HILL
MAY 17, 1995

Upon a hill he died for me
Overlooking the city wall
He died, He died to save just me
On the cross of Calvary

Upon a hill He ascended
To His throne divine
Prepared by His Father
To rule at His right hand

Upon a Hill He will come
To His temple to rule and reign
Then the earth shall rest in peace
When He comes again in glory

Upon a Hill, He died for me
So I too could go back to Father
He makes my state clean and pure
As I partake of His gentle mercy

Upon a Hill, He will remain
To rule throughout eternity
So all can kneel and adore
Their King and Savior evermore

Upon a Hill, I will ascend
To greet Him, who died for me
I will bow and kiss His feet
Rejoicing at His coming

Upon a Hill, I will sing
Hosannas to His name
All hail to may Lord and Savior
Jesus, My everlasting King

AMEN

## ME, AN INSTRUMENT OF PEACE

MAY 18, 1995

Can I be an instrument of Peace?
Can I put away angry thoughts?
Can I change a most imperfect me?
Can I emulate joyfulness in what I say and do?

Can I just walk with the Master?
Can I, day by day, heal my very soul?
Can I do what is right no matter What?
Can I just love my children?

Can I let them be them?
Can I guide them with Wisdom?
Can I teach them with kindness?
Can I just be there when they need me?

And the Lord answers:

Yes, Karen, you can be all of these
I will teach you each day
Just listen to the whisperings of the spirit

The whisperings of encouragement
The whisperings of long lost hope
The whisperings of a daughter's prayer

The whisperings of the birds chirping
The whisperings of a trickle of water
The whisperings of a whining dog

The whisperings of a slow sluggish snail
The whisperings of a flower in bloom
The whisperings of a rainbow

The whisperings of lightning and thunder
The whisperings of a dew mist on mossy grass
The whisperings of a calm lake

The whisperings of a river ever flowing
The whisperings of an age-old tree
The whisperings of a husband's prayer

The whisperings of the scriptures
The whisperings of a mother's prayer
The whisperings of the sweet Holy Spirit

JUST LISTEN KAREN

YOU CAN BE AN INSTRUMENT OF PEACE

## MORNING BECKONS

JUNE 9, 1995

Morning puts her fingers on my brow
I stretch and yawn to greet her
Then I curl back up in the arms of my blanket

I squint my eyes to say hello
She beckons me to come and partake
Then a finger, a head, a toe peeks out

Good Morning – Morning, I say
It's a new day in the Lord
I love all the sounds of morning

Morning brings the chirping of nestling birds
It brings the sun peeking through fluffy clouds
It brings a sweet hello from heaven above

Morning stretches her fingers, hello
Come to greet me with your smile
And I will give you comfort of a new day

## CREATING ANEW

June 9, 1995

A new mortal to create
Though a sinful past
Jesus, touches me, a sinner

He says, let's create anew
A soul worth all the gold
So she can bless and multiply my love

So we create a mortal
New and bright, clean and pure
To magnify Our Father in Heaven

As 1 bow on bended knee
I thank the Lord for Jesus
Now I can hold my head up high

He allows me to create anew
A spirit so stifled from the past
Now a brilliant path to redeem

A new mortal to create
Step by step, inch by inch
Jesus, He touches me, a sinner

## I GO MY WAY

### June 18, 1995

I go and go my way
I get lost, lost on my way
My head hangs low

A voice whispers come back
I turn and listen again
Come back, my daughter

Then I put one foot on the path
I take a step with a tear
Then I walk toward the voice

Each step, tears keep streaming
Then I run to Him who died for me
And I sit at His feet

I beg for mercy for wayward ways
He touches my head
He forgives me and shows me another path

I go down the new path trembling
I look back and He smiles at me
So, He says, you'll find joy

As I walk, my knees knock
I stay on the straight path
A path with pebbles and bridges

Flowers adorn this path
Some with thorns and some not
However, I stay and fall on my knees

He then comes and walks beside me
Now I can walk a straight line
Piece by piece, I can purify my mind

Like peeling an orange
My old self is left behind
I can be a new fruit

As I walk on His path
Now I go His way
A way to celestial destiny
My friends help me with His way
Your way is much better, Lord
May I keep my eyes on the new path

I come unto you, Lord
A vessel filled with joy
To walk in your ways all my days

## A VEIL OF FOG

January 25, 1997

Fog created over our minds
To place us on earth without memory
Sometimes – I catch a glimpse of home
Then I yearn to go back quickly

Oh Father, I plead, don't forget me down here
Then I feel a warmth around my arms
Angels attending me as I walk on earth
To help me on my journey of mortality

This fog hurts my head so much
Because – I want to remember
When do I get a glimpse of light?
I feel so inadequate to my spiritual self

Then I must talk with myself
It's okay to learn in your mortal body
Be patient with yourself
The spirit knows what you can accomplish

Though the veil of fog is present
The spirit within you knows life
It will guide your body to do great things
With the help of the Lord

The fog will be lifted
When mortality draws nigh
Your friends and family will greet you
Welcome home, welcome home, welcome home

## MY FATHER
### December 6, 1997

My Daddy, Who loved me

Before I came to be

He swung me, He cradled me

Daddy, Oh Daddy

Swing me high, swing me low

Daddy let me come with you

Hands in his pockets

Hands in my pockets

Walking side by side

Not a sound of voice

Walking in perfect harmony

Daddy, teach me about God

Daddy took me to church

He was an altar boy

He sang in choir

A beautiful voice

Daddy, daddy, don't leave me here

Oh, I must go, he said

I will be your guardian

And so my Daddy is

## LITTLE EAGLES
FEBRUARY 22, 1999

Little eagles wake up with life on their lips
Little eagles play and play until they nestle
their heads in a soft pillow
Little eagles forgive a hurt as soon as it is given
Little eagles have blue, dark brown, and pale green eyes
Little eagles wear their many faces without a mask
Little eagles soar to heaven for their counsel
Little eagles teach adult eagles
many sacred things
Little eagles have complete faith in God
Little eagles depend on us to teach them too.
Little eagles of today are the eagles of tomorrow

## **ENJOY THE DAYLIGHT OF YOUR LIFE**
### February 2, 1999

Let the sun shine upon my head
Rejoice in the daylight
Laugh through the darkness
Let the light shine upon your lips

Play the journey of life
Fulfill your dreams with passion
Heart-filled exuberant force
Enjoy the daylight of your life

Give God a hand for His goodness
Rejoice in His infinite compassion and mercy
Dance to the beat of your drum
Hang on to you, laugh, cry, pray, and dance

Enjoy the daylight of your life
Take hold — Grasp it tight
You are the difference
Rejoice in you!

God made you

You are His child

I am His child

Alleluia — He loves me any old way


All right – – Enjoy

The daylight of your Life

I will – – God gave it to me


AMEN

## YOU DON'T HAVE TO WALK IN MY FOOTSTEPS
### February 2, 1999

You don't have to walk in my footsteps
I invite you to walk beside me
Laugh, giggle, play, dance, cry

Let me show you a part of my world
Tickle your toes in the icy cold waters of the ocean
Crunch your bare feet in the cool lush carpet of grass

Take a sponge and dip it into the paint and dab dab dab
Twirl and dance, lift your feet and raise your hands
Swinging to the tune of the joyous music

Sing a little song of joyful sounds
Rush, rush, rush to see the flowers bloom
Come, come with me and share my life

## SMILE

August 6, 1987

Choose ye this day to be happy
Smile brings a smile
Kindness generates love
Glow from within and be Happy

Oh, ye people repent of frowns
They have no place in God's kingdom
Though destitute rejoice in the Lord
For He is ever at your side

Mortality and all its cares
Are but fleeting moments of eternity
So rejoice all you saints
Be happy and have a light heart

## **BLENDING OF THE COLORS**
### August 2, 1987

We are the artists of our lives
Choices of colors to blend
To multiply the love
That God has for us

A rainbow, we can create
From early morn to silver dusk
Spreading sunshine to all we meet
Is our gift to our Father

Wrapping ourselves in self-control
Is to be like the Master artist
Blending all the colors of virtue
To kneel and adore at His throne

## **A GIFT OF THE SOUL**
### September 7, 1987

Writing, a gift of the soul
Given to me to quench all desires
And to bless all who will hear

May this gift be multiplied
So that many will be inspired
To write and also be fulfilled

Writing, a blessing unto me
To share all that is within
And to give praise unto God

## CONCLUSION OF PART I
### THE JOURNEY OF AN EAGLE

As I reflect on the journey of an Eagle, I say, the journey continues. There are more chapters to write as I live. So, pondering the wind, the turbulence, the calm and peaceful time, I have written another poem about gliding when the winds come. When I fight or flutter against the wind, I am exhausted. I have no energy to complete that very hour or day or, how about that very minute. So now I glide when the turbulence and winds come to lift me. Sometimes, they bring me to a peaceful shore and sometimes I must fly strong like an Eagle to a safer place.

Now in my autumn years, I enjoy my journey as it comes moment after each moment. Oh, I could wish my days away and dream of a future full of wealth and excitement but I choose not to do this. Enjoy this moment; take notice of it and live it to the fullest. NOW is the key. It is all I have, RIGHT NOW. So my life is full of the laughter of little children, – as well as mine, play time, study time, meditation and prayer time, composing time, gardening time, cleaning time, writing time, dancing and singing time, and the list goes on and on for me because I love to do almost everything.

I say thank you to my Heavenly Father for His constant love, protection, help, support, and counsel that He gives me. I feel It! Is warmth like a cozy, velvety blanket all wrapped around me on a cool day, that covers my whole being.

May each of you who read this book be blessed. May your journey on Earth be an EAGLE one.

Spread your wings and fly. Do what your heart tells you to do. Follow the God in you to be the very best you. I promise you, there is a rainbow out there, just waiting to catch your eye. Help another soul. Just smile, or give an embrace or do something for someone else and you will feel God in you. You will soar like an Eagle.

Thanks to all my family and friends who have helped me on my journey. Thanks to my enemies too. Because without them, I could not see the opposite point of view. Sometimes my friends were my enemies. What this taught me was forgiveness. The very growth of my soul may be because of my enemies. Well, anyway, I thank all of you for being there on the path when I was there also. Love and blessings to you all.

## WIND FOR AN EAGLE
### May 14, 1999

If you want to be an eagle

The wind is your friend

It helps you with your journey


Soaring or coasting is necessary

So when you have to fly

You can make it with more ease


Flying against all odds is hard

Then the wind comes to lift you

To make your journey less difficult

The wind is my friend
It whispers coolness
Against my sun-beaten brow

As I walk in this life
I stretch my arms out
So I can feel the cool brisk wmd

I twirl and twirl under the trees
As the wind blows through my hair
Cooling my hot-soaked body

Oh yes, If you are an Eagle
The wind is your friend
To help you on your journey

# THE JOURNEY OF AN EAGLE
## PART II
### WHERE MERCY AND LOVE ABOUND

My journey, as it continues, directs me on the path of Love and Mercy.

It puzzles me during this part of my life, that these two attributes would become front and center. My experiences of this year have been testing grounds of these attributes. I will give you examples of these experiences.

When I wanted to have my grandson leave our home, there was a voice inside of me that said, "Karen, have mercy and compassion on him." So, as we struggle with his lifestyle, we are taught love and compassion by the Lord. I don't know what happened to him in his early childhood to convince him that he is gay.

I am sad in my heart for him as I watch him struggle for his identity. So, as a result, we have allowed him to stay in our home.

One of my daughters is still living with us. She struggles to be independent from us and doesn't want to live alone. She's going to have a baby soon.

I can hardly wait to pick up that wee one in my arms. She's going to be a good mom. He comes with his own self-reliant spirit. He is a strong spirit like his mother. It takes a lot of love and compassion and certainly mercy to have her in our home. She has a fiery spirit. So, sometimes it is uncomfortable to be around her. Then, there are those special times when we talk and really communicate with love and understanding. She helps me a lot sometimes. She helps me to face me. She is one of my many mirrors. It is uncomfortable sometimes but I hang in there because she is so important to me. I love to hear her giggle and laugh when she is on the phone. Her laughter echoes through the whole house, creating such joy in our hearts. It makes me want to laugh too. Jimmy and I sit in our bed and chuckle as we listen to her laugh.

Now onto a different example of my experience with love and mercy. MMM… this is really tough but I will continue.

I will start out by saying that without forgiveness, we can't have mercy.

I was not too merciful unto my mother in her last days on earth. I didn't know these were her last days. Maybe, I would have acted differently, I just don't know. So, I chose to deal with her brother's predator behavior towards us girls. She always protected him even if he was wrong. She excused him always. It finally made me so angry that I wrote a letter to her. I told her about his behavior and how I got tired of hearing her excuses for it.

Also, I told her if she still wanted to control my life with her money and things that I wanted no part of it. I sent the artwork back to her that she sent me. I was so angry that I couldn't see the hurt I would cause because of my foggy vision. However, all this didn't mean that I didn't want any tokens of hers when she left the earth.

Well, the Lord worked on my heart after I did all this. One day, a whisper came to me to write an apology note. I listened and I wrote one. Mother wrote me back to thank me. The hurt was still there. I called Mom on Tuesday before she died on Sunday. We had a good talk but not like before.

Our whole relationship was not resolved when she lay in the grave. Oh mom, I am sorry. Tears of anguish rolling down my cheek. If only I could have five more minutes with her on a conscious level. We could hug and cry in each other's arms.

So now, I pray that mom can have peace on the other side of the veil as she sorts out her anger. I pray every day for her. When I receive peace in my heart that she has forgiven my anger towards her and her acceptance of her brother's perversion, then I will stop praying for her peace because she will have it. I am not so blind that I can't see her anguish. Life continues on the other side. Sometimes, people are happy and sometimes they are sad. I feel mom is both sometimes. She will be ok.

All I have to say to her is, "Mom, I love you. I forgive you, and I cherish you. I am crying with you. I am healing with you." Without the great mercy and love of God, we both would hurt so much more. He has helped me each day to grieve less and live more. Now, I can hardly wait to embrace my mother and tell her that I love her.

So my journey continues as I learn about mercy and love. Two little attributes just waiting for someone to hold their hands and walk through life.

My prayer is: "Father, help me to love more and more mercy. Let me see, how the other person feels before I rant and rave. Let me be still and hear your voice. Help me, Father, help me to be more like you."

I have created poems concerning my feelings on mercy and love. May just one touch your heart and fill your soul with compassion and love.

## ACROSS THE VEIL
### August 16, 2002

As I stretch my soul to cross the veil
I hear a spirit weeping ---
I cry too as I hear my mother
Mourning the loss of her body
It's ok—Mom—Daddy is there
Lean on him to help you
She pushes away—angry to be dead
Then her hands fill up with tears
Jesus comes along and embraces her
Her tears are wiped by His gentle hands
No need to cry ---
The pain of earth life will soon disappear
They walk and talk --- she is comforted
Love and Mercy abide here, He says
You'll forgive and she'll forgive
And mercy and love will endure.
Then I see her smile ---
As she watches me have peace
I wish that I could speak to her
She wishes that she could speak to me
We will one day speak

With love and Mercy on our lips
We will both heal ---
from the wounds of yesterday
They are but memories on our faces
Love is spoken in our hearts
So we both can continue our lives
Journeys of happiness and joy
As we make our lives simple
In the love of God
Peace will abound as love and mercy reign

## AN EAGLE SOARS
### July 24, 2002

An Eagle soars into the heavens
Watching all her loved ones
Hoping they will help each other

Oh, how different are my eagles
Will they set aside their differences
and take the time to love each other?

My children, My children
The Eagle cries from above
Listen to your hearts and Love

One hears her voice, then another
Ok Mom – we will love each other
We will embrace your tender ones

An Eagle soars and glides
Watching all her loved ones
Helping each other grow

## MOM AND DAD LIVE

JULY 23, 2002

Mom crossed the veil
Hand and Hand with Daddy
To meet Her eternal Savior

Now their lives are memories
We must live what they taught us
To be close to Jesus and Do His works

Though tears are wet upon our faces
We must continue our Journey
We must cherish and Love Each Other

Mom and Dad live across the veil now
Praying and preparing for us
To return home safely to our living Savior

## COMFORT AND PEACE
### July 22, 2002

I feel the sweet peace
Of our Savior's radiant smile
As He watches me grow into me

So much work to do on me
One Step at a time
Comes a familiar whisper

.

Working on Love and Mercy
Attributes to cherish
To make my spirit soar

Oh Jesus, comfort my soul
Anguished by my temper
Sorrowed by my evil words

Please forgive me
Please forgive me
Is my plea

Then the sweet comfort
Of peaceful words
Flood my torn soul

Be quiet, Karen, Be still
Just another thing to work on
As you go each day to live

As you trust in Me
You will be a calm spirit
And you shall have eternal peace

You are growing into you
I am smiling upon you
I will grant you comfort and peace

## **LISTEN TO MY HEART**

AUGUST 17, 2002

Mother, oh Mother
Listen to my heart
I was telling you how important you are to me
My anger clouded my meaning
Your anger clouded my words
Things and money weren't important to me
I would rather have you to walk beside
I would rather have you to talk to
You were my friend
And counselor
Not only my mother;
Who bore me
Mother, Mother taxes can wait
I want to see you, Please
Please Mother reach out your heart to me
Let me come and visit
So I can feel your soft face
Cradled around my neck as we embrace
Mother, Oh Mother
listen to my heart
You are very important to me.

## **WHAT'S YOUR HURRY**

July 24, 2002

HURRY, HURRY, HURRY!
Where are you going?
Brake—Pause—Listen
Do you hear it?
Do you see it?

The Birds are chirping
The leaves are rustling
The wind is singing
The flowers are dancing
The clouds are forming
The trees are whipering
The rain is prancing
The Snow is glimmering
The Sun is glowing
The Moon is waking
The Stars are shooting
People are laughing
The Baby is crying
The children are playing
Your heart is beating
Your feet are walking
Your brain is thinking
The ant is working
The Bee is buzzing
The Frog is croaking

So what's your hurry?
Enjoy the life around you
Brake—Pause—Listen

## TAKE TIME

JULY 24, 2002

Take time to pick up a new infant
And smell the newness of life
Feel the soft, tender skin
As it glides by your cheek

Take time to smell a rose
With its petals so soft
Like the skin of a new baby
And its newness of life

Take time to play with a dog
So full of energy and life
Like the cries of a baby
Come play with me, come play with me

Take time to walk
Along a great calm lake
Like a baby sleeping
In the arms of its mother

Take time to say I love you
Giving hugs and kisses freely
To all those you love
As you do when you hold a newborn baby

## **JESUS SPEAKS TO MY HEART**
### August 17, 2002

Forgive, and I shall have mercy on you
Forgive not and I shall not forgive you
As you walk beside me
You shall learn to be gentle
You will learn to have compassion
You will leave worldly things behind

You will live a simple, sweet life
Love and Mercy will be in your heart
Rest your mind in my bosom
Quenching your brow with living water
Quiet—Forgive—Pray—Be Still
Forgive, and I shall have mercy on you

Karen Marie Berard Miño

## MY GOAL TO BE GENTLE AGAIN
### AUGUST 17, 2002

Once — when I was born
I was a gentle, sweet soul
As life continued
I became soft in a shell
Like a clam,
Vulnerable to pecking

As I grew older
I learned to carry a sword
Sometimes at my side
Other times drawn to capacity
May I put my sword aside
So Jesus can teach me
a gentle way
It's scary to put my sword down
And yet a voice says — it's time

It's time to walk beside me
It's time to live a gentle life
It's time to caress time
It's time to be — just be

Your spirit can be gentle again
As you walk in the Savior's light
Your spirit will develop calmness
As an Eagle gliding through the air.

## GOD HAS A PLAN FOR THEE
August 17, 2002

Arise, Oh my Soul
God has a plan for thee
Companions — Love and Mercy
To be yours forever

Worlds to see and experience
People to share Truth
Your companions
Love and Mercy
Journey with you now

Arise, Oh my Soul
God has a plan for thee
Love and Mercy
await your arrival
On the Threshold of Life

## CONCLUSION OF PART II

Love and Mercy abound in the Righteous heart.

They are not Easy attributes to have in your Life. They are worth the effort to apply in your life. Your life will be guided in a new light as you Apply love and mercy to it.

## ABOUT THE AUTHOR

Karen Marie Berard Miño was born in Spokane, Washington on November 9, 1947. She grew up in staunch Catholic home. Karen went to Catholic school for twelve years.

She married her high school sweetheart. From this marriage, she received two beautiful sons, Daniel and Kenneth. She stayed in this marriage for seven years.

Karen then married Jaime E. Miño. They have been married for thirty years. They have four beautiful daughters, Katherine, Karen, Mary and Jamie. They have nineteen grand children and seven grand children

Karen loves many different things. She loves to waitress. She has a talent in Massage work. She loves to garden. She loves to create beauty wherever she goes

Her garden is her saving grace. Taught by many mentors — Grandpa Abb, Rose Stone, and many more — how to nurture plants and help them grow, she can create beauty out of bare earth. Digging in the soil helps the pain go away. She could feel it slip into the earth as she was digging in it.

The pain, oh the pain. How it hurt her. She would swim and swim day after day until she felt clean and pure. Could she wash all that gunk off her spirit by swimming? She tried and tried to no avail. She just felt dirty all the time, so she prayed and cried to God, "HELP ME TO FEEL CLEAN AND PURE!" One day, He just poured His Spirit over her. She felt bathed in His light and washed clean from the ugliness of yester years of so many violations against her.

Today, Karen, is a composer, author, speaker, nanny, wife, mother, grandma, gardener, scholar and a dancer. Karen loves to do many things. The busier she is, the happier she is and yet she can enjoy the solitude of nature and ponder life while listening to the echoes of birds, leaves falling, flowers blooming, bees buzzing, waves crashing, trees laughing, and little animals scattering.

She now feels that she needs to educate her family and others about safe touch. How can we keep our children safe? How can we educate them and their parents, and clergy members? These are just some of the questions she asks herself. She is actively supporting safe environments in church buildings. There needs to be windows on all primary-age children's doors. That is her feeling anyway. This would protect the children and the adults.

# Love Reaches To My Inner Child

# LOVE REACHES THROUGH ETERNITY